PICK A PATH TO ADVENTURE™

You are Chaylo. As a reward for catching an enemy spy, you and your fellow Star Rangers are on a tour of Space Fleet's new SOLAR Star Station. When disaster strikes, the sight-seeing is over, but the fun begins!

You might be a kid, but you're brave and smart—smart enough to stay out of trouble . . . you hope!

SOL, the huge SOLAR Robot, has gone haywire and escaped from the Robot Test Area. Now he's blasting the whole station with energy bolts. Someone has to stop him!

Will you jump through the hole the monster robot made in the wall and chase after him?

Or do you want to pull the little green alien out of the pond and ask for his help?

The choice is yours!

FANTASY FOREST™

8

PICK A PATH TO ADVENTURE™

BOOKS

Star Rangers Meet The Solar Robot

by Beverly Charette
and
Mario D. Macari

Cover and Interior Illustrations by
Mario D. Macari

TSR, Inc.
PRODUCTS OF YOUR IMAGINATION™

Stop!

Don't turn this page yet!

You're about to set out on not one, but many great adventures in the Frontier of space! Here's all you have to do—

To start your adventure, turn to page 7 and begin. Read until you come to a set of choices. Pick one and follow the directions.
As you read, keep making choices and following directions until the story ends. Then start at the beginning again and pick other choices. Each one will take you on a different adventure.

All right, go ahead and turn the page . . .

"Identification, please!" a mechanical voice orders. A huge yellow robot marked SECURITY looks at you fiercely.

You quickly hold up your visitor's card and walk down the ramp from the shuttle. The eye sensors of the robot glow red as they scan the card. For just a second you're afraid he's going to stop you.

But then he beeps, "Approved. Next."

The other excited Star Rangers join you.

"He gives me the creeps," you say, pointing back to the robot.

"Me, too," says your Yazirian friend, Rama. "But he's supposed to look scary— he's a security bot."

Rama presses her monkeylike face to a window above the main lobby of the space station and whistles. "It's so big!"

"It looks more like a whole planet than a man-made star station," says Gogol. The Dralasite scratches his rubbery head.

"What a field trip!" you exclaim.

"Admiral Shuk was very generous to give you this trip as a reward for stopping the Sathar spy," beeps Nanny Navigator Robot.

You nod but secretly wish your guardian robot didn't always have to come with you.

"Someone should design shuttle seats to fit eight legs," grumbles Carell. "We Vrusks just don't have enough leg room!"

A tall, dark human walks up to you and smiles. "Welcome to the SOLAR Star Station. I'm Commander Brant."

You and your Star Ranger friends salute. As leader, you say, "It's an honor to meet you, sir." You shake his hand.

"The honor's mine. Congratulations on capturing the spy at Space Fleet."

"Well, uh, thank you, sir." You feel your face grow red.

"Now, we've got lots to show you," he says. "Let's get started."

You all step out into a huge mall.

"The SOLAR Star Station is really just a great city floating in space," Brant explains. "Yet each major area is independent, with an emergency escape air lock of its own."

He points to a model of the station. It looks to you like two pyramids joined together at their points.

"But, sir, what does SOLAR stand for?"

Carell asks. The Vrusk is always curious.

"*Strategic Orbiting Laboratories for Astronomical Research,*" Commander Brant replies. "Do you know what that means?"

"Studying stars and planets?" you ask.

"Right!" Commander Brant smiles.

"What's that over there?" Gogol asks, pointing at a crowded exhibit.

"Come and look," Brant says.

You squirm to the front of the crowd.

A tiny cube-shaped creature you recognize as a Boxil is saying, "Welcome to Light

World." It points to one of the ugliest creatures you've ever seen!

"Ugh!" cries Gogol. "What is that slimy, froglike thing?"

Rama says, "I've seen a criggle before. What's so special about that?"

Carell winks at you. "I dare you to touch it, Rama," he says.

Rama looks closely at the criggle. It has many arms and hundreds of tiny teeth. It sits in a puddle of green slime. Rama glances at the waiting crowd, gulps, and quickly reaches out her hand.

But instead of touching the creature, her hand goes right through it!

"Hey, she missed it!" Gogol says as you and Carell chuckle.

"No, she didn't," says Carell, "because it's not there. It's a hologram."

"What-o-gram?" asks Gogol.

"A hologram," you pipe up.

"A hologram is like a photograph, only it's three-dimensional. It's a picture made with laser light," Carell explains.

"The thing you take a picture of looks as if it's sitting right in front of you. You can walk around it," you add.

Gogol imitates Rama's voice: "What's so special about that?"

Rama pulls back her arm to punch Gogol, but a SQUAWK! on the commander's wrist radio interrupts. "Commander, we've got some trouble in the computer room," a voice says.

"What sort of trouble?" Brant asks.

You hear the voice gulp and then say, "Well, uh, it's an explosion, sir."

"WHAT!" Brant explodes himself.

Just then you turn and see the big security robot roll past you, waving its arms strangely. "That's odd," you think. "I wonder if he's supposed to be doing that."

Commander Brant sighs. "Well, it looks as if we'll have to take a side trip to the computer room. I hope you don't mind."

If you quickly follow Commander Brant to the computer room, turn to page 15.

If you decide to take time to tell Commander Brant about the robot's strange actions, turn to page 45.

As you pass through the heavy double doors of the computer room, you see scientists in white lab coats scurrying about in a panic. A big computer terminal sparks wildly, and smelly black smoke curls toward the ceiling.

"What's going on?" Brant demands.

But before anyone can answer, KAPOW! an energy beam zaps from nowhere, and a man falls to the floor, stunned.

BLAM! another blast hits the wall behind you, and you dive for cover. Humans crouch behind tables. Robots circle in confusion.

As the smoke clears, you can see a nine-foot-tall robot soldier standing in front of the damaged terminal with his arms crossed.

"Who are you?" Commander Brant demands, taking a step forward. "What do you want?"

The mechanical soldier says nothing. But from his middle section, more energy bolts blast the room. A stray shot hits Nanny Robot, and she short-circuits with a puff of smoke. Her head tilts to one side.

"Nanny!" you cry to your guardian.

"Everyone to the hall!" Brant shouts.

Humans and robots rush from the room. You grab Nanny Robot and roll her out just as more blasts zap the closing double doors.

In the hall, you and the other Star Rangers look sadly at your broken robot.

"That rotten soldier!" growls Rama.

"Security!" Brant shouts into an intercom by the door. "What's going on?"

From the wall speaker, you hear a timid voice reply, "I don't know, sir. There are robot soldiers everywhere! I don't know where from." The voice gasps. "They've taken over the Life Support Room!"

The commander bellows, "Security Chief Swift report to the Life Support Room now!"

Then he sighs and quietly adds, "All computer personnel report to the Bypass Room. Small back-up computers will run the station until we can fix the main one."

Rama says to you, "Let's help!"

If you want to help in the Life Support Room, turn to page 18.

If you think you could be more helpful in the Bypass Room, turn to page 34.

"Everyone needs to keep breathing," you say. "So Chief Swift may need help in the Life Support Room."

"All right!" cries Rama and the others. "Which way to the Life Support Room?"

Brant quickly tells you how to find the room. "But stay well away from the line of fire," he adds. "Those energy blasts might only stun an adult, but **you** could get hurt."

"Yes, sir!" you promise.

You turn into a narrow hallway. A group of guards walks ahead of you. A whooshing sound makes one guard turn. "Look out!"

You jump to the wall as a yellow robot that almost fills the hall rolls past.

"That's the robot that checked us into the star station," you say, jumping up.

"SOL, the SOLAR Robot, was made just for our security force," the closest guard explains. "He's probably been called by Chief Swift."

The guards lead you around a corner. Directly ahead of you are tall doors marked LIFE SUPPORT ROOM. As you watch, Sol rolls through the doors. They close, and two robot soldiers step in front of them.

Up and down the hall, security guards crouch behind boxes for protection. You see SWIFT written on one guard's uniform.

"SOL!" he calls. "Come out of there!"

"Chief Swi—" you start to say.

"THIS IS SOL!" You jump at the boom of a mechanical voice. On an overhead video screen, you see the yellow robot's face.

"I am taking over this Star Station. Attempts to interfere will be met by my soldiers." Energy bolts zap toward the guards, who scatter.

You and Gogol duck around a corner, as

Carell and Rama run down another hall.

Looking around for a place to hide, you spot an air duct from the Life Support Room. It's big enough to crawl through but pretty high. Down the hall is a door marked LOCKER ROOM.

If you decide to crawl into the air duct and hide, turn to page 23.

If you'd rather hide in the locker room, turn to page 26.

"They won't be able to get us if we're in that air duct!" you say. You leap for the grating, but your fingers don't reach it.

"I wish my arms were longer," you moan.

Gogol proudly exclaims, "Humans can't stretch, but Dralasites can!"

He shuts his eyes, concentrating. Then his arms, stretched long and thin, snake up to the air duct. He quickly unlatches the grating.

You pull yourself up Gogol's arms and crawl inside the air duct.

You hold Gogol's hands on the grating as his arms shrink, and he draws his body toward the duct. You pull your friend inside.

Suddenly, SOL's voice booms out, "Now I get to do what I want to do!"

"That's SOL in the Life Support Room!" you whisper. Then an idea comes to you. "Gogol, maybe we can get in there and open the door for Chief Swift and his guards."

"Are you nuts?" Gogol says aloud.

"Shhhh! Remember—we said we were going to help."

Gogol's rubbery face frowns, but he shrugs and says, "Lead on."

Soon you reach a grating where you can look down into the Life Support Room. SOL stands at a huge control board. As he punches some buttons, he mutters, "I'll show them!"

Gogol leans over to see, too. There's a click and he tumbles through the grating!

"Oh, noooo!" he cries as he lands with a THUD! The robot spins around and sees the young Dralasite sprawled on the floor.

"So," SOL sneers, "you want to trick the master robot! I'll show you a trick I can do with energy bolts!" He points a huge arm at Gogol.

Gogol whimpers. What will you do?

You could jump down on SOL from the duct. But he's so big—would it do any good? Maybe you can drop to the control panel and find the buttons that open the doors.

Will you attack SOL to save Gogol? If this is your choice, turn to page 40.

Or will you run to open the door and let Chief Swift and his guards save your friend? Turn to page 42.

You're too scared to waste time climbing into an air duct. You just want to hide.

"Come on, Gogol!" you shout as you run for the locker room.

As the door closes behind you, you see lockers filled with spacesuits, helmets, and jetpacks, all in different sizes. On the far wall is a door marked DECOMPRESSION CHAMBER.

"This must be the main air lock," you say, puffing from your run. "It looks just like the one at Space Fleet Command."

"Commander Brant did say that each major area on the star station has an emergency air lock," Gogol comments.

Instantly you're struck by an idea. "Gogol, we could get into the Life Support Room through its air lock!" you say.

"Maybe we can help stop that mad robot!" Gogol adds excitedly.

You find a spacesuit that fits while the Dralasite slips into a suit. Then you both step into the air lock.

As the air is drawn from the compartment, you feel a little afraid, but you know that you

are doing the right thing . . . don't you?

Moments later, the lock releases, and the two of you step away from the slowly rotating star station. Laughing with delight, you somersault, enjoying the feeling of being weightless.

Suddenly, shrill laughter broadcasts over your suit radio. "I've been watching you from the moment you entered the air lock," a metallic voice snarls. You look up and see SOL through a window.

"That must be the Life Support Room," says Gogol with a shaky voice.

"You don't scare me, you bucket of bolts!" you shout, though you wish you felt as brave as you sound.

"I don't?" booms SOL with an evil chuckle. "Then maybe my pet will!"

Puzzled by his words, you use your jet pack to turn around. The hairs on your neck stand straight up!

There, floating in space, is the ugliest, most terrifying monster you've ever seen! It's huge and slimy-looking. Its black lips curl back in a snarl and reveal hundreds of razor-sharp teeth!

"Oh!" gasps Gogol.

"Wait a minute," you whisper to Gogol. "I think I've seen that creature before. And it wasn't so horrible. But where was it?"

Will you stand your ground and fight the beast? If so, turn to page 30.

Or will you make a break for the hatch to the space locker room? Turn to page 44.

You raise your arms to strike the beast in the face but suddenly remember where you saw this creature before. "Jetpack, Gogol!" The small thrusters on your pack send you to the hatch for the Life Support Room air lock.

"Are you crazy?" Gogol cries as the beast reaches toward you. Its growl grows louder on your radio speaker.

"Ignore it," you say calmly. "It can't hurt us—it's a hologram. Remember the creature we saw in the mall exhibit?"

Gogol, scarcely breathing, peeks back. "Oh yeah," he admits, "now that you mention

it, the two creatures do look sort of alike."

"And the only way that SOL can control the beast and make it roar over our suit radios is through the computer," you add, pressing a button by the air lock.

Through the window you can see SOL waving his arms furiously. "Stop them, my pet!" the robot commands.

For just a second you fear the monster is real after all! But then the image of its claw passes through you. You and Gogol enter the air lock, laughing with relief.

When a light shows that the room is filled

with air, you take off your helmets and get ready to run to the door. But when the air lock opens, you find Chief Swift and Commander Brant waiting for you.

"We've stopped SOL, thanks to you!"

Your mouth drops open in surprise.

"SOL was so busy trying to scare you two, he forgot about us," says Swift.

"All over the star station," Brant continues, "the evil soldiers began to fade. They were holograms! And their energy bolts were laser beams controlled by SOL."

"Because you distracted SOL," says Swift, "we were able to sneak up and disconnect his energy source."

"Space Fleet is once again in the Star Rangers' debt," Commander Brant says. "If there's anything we can do . . ."

You look at SOL standing limp and quiet and say, "Well, we'd like to have Nanny Robot back in working order." Gogol nods.

"She nags us sometimes," you add, "but it is nice to have her around."

THE END

"Commander Brant will probably want us to go to the Bypass Room where it's less dangerous," you tell the others.

Brant stops speaking on the intercom and you say, "Excuse me, sir, but we Star Rangers know something about computers. Maybe we can help in the Bypass Room."

"Good idea! Just follow that group of scientists . . . and be careful!"

The four of you join a group of scientists hurrying toward the Bypass Room. As usual, you and Rama race ahead.

Falling into step with a woman in a white lab coat, you say, "My name's Chaylo, ma'am, and this is Rama."

"Star Rangers," she says with a smile. "I was a Star Ranger once. I'm Dr. Walden."

"What's happening?" you ask.

"I'm not really sure," she replies. "I was working when I heard a commotion outside my office. I opened the door and saw one of those sold—"

The floor suddenly starts to shake.

"What's that?" Rama moves closer to you.

A huge yellow robot rolls into view. It's the same robot you saw when you first arrived.

"That's SOL, the SOLAR Robot," Dr. Walden says with a smile.

"SOL?" you repeat. "He looks mean."

Dr. Walden nods. "He was built as a security bot to guard the station."

"I'm glad he's on duty," says Rama. "Maybe he'll get rid of those soldiers."

The SOLAR Robot wheels up to you and the scientists. He lifts his hand, and you think he's going to shake yours. But instead, flaming bolts of energy fire from his fingertips. The scientists scatter, Carell and Gogol with them.

"Chaylo! Here!" Rama grabs your hand.

Running hard to dodge the robot's energy bolts, you and Rama turn a corner.

"That was close!" you say, panting.

"Why would a bot go crazy?" Rama asks.

"I don't know," you reply. Then you look up and see a door with a sign that reads ROBOT WORKSHOP.

"But maybe we can get an answer in there." You start to walk toward the door.

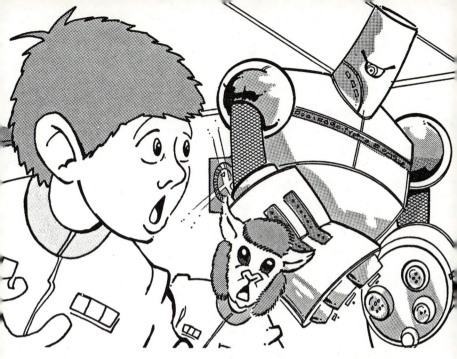

"Chaylo..." Something in Rama's voice makes you turn toward her.

Towering above you, silver and gleaming, is the tallest, meanest-looking robot soldier you've ever imagined!

He has no eyes or mouth, just a blinking red light for a face. He moves toward you.

Do you want to try and fight the soldier? Turn to page 38.

Or do you want to make a run for it into the robot workshop? Turn to page 49.

"You're not getting me without a fight!" You rush toward the soldier robot.

WHOOOOOSHHH!

THUMP! You hit the opposite wall. You didn't dodge the soldier, you went right through him!

Rama stares at him blankly. She slowly reaches out to touch the soldier, but her hand passes through!

"A hologram!" you both say together.

"Exactly!" A green alien in a fishbowl helmet peeks around the corner.

"Who are you?" you ask suspiciously.

"Sniksil's my name, Robotics, my game." He places his hand over a light sensor on the wall, and the soldier disappears.

"Sniksil!" Rama says angrily. "Did you create these evil soldiers?"

The little alien steps back and says, "Dear me! I should say not!"

He walks over to a door marked ROBOT WORKSHOP, opens it, and steps inside. You and Rama rush after him.

Please turn to page 64.

"No!" you shout from the air duct.

"Ah!" SOL looks up. "My sensors did show another life form in this room." He laughs. "Don't worry, you're next!"

Trembling, you jump out of the duct.

You land on SOL's shoulder and start beating his metal head with your fists, but a sweep of his arm sends you to the floor.

You're glad to see that Gogol had time to get out of the way.

As SOL turns his blasters toward you, you grab a wrench on a nearby desk and throw it with all your might.

CLANG! it hits SOL's mouth speaker. Then with buzzes and pops, his head starts spinning, and sparks spray the room.

The big double doors burst open.

"What's going on in here?" Chief Swift demands. He aims his blaster at SOL, but the sparks fizzle out, and the robot stands still.

Chief Swift picks up the wrench.

"Here," he says, smiling. "You might want to keep this as a souvenir. The Star Rangers have saved the day!"

THE END

You drop from the air duct to the floor and scramble for protection behind a chair next to the control board.

"Another enemy life form?" SOL roars. His eye sensors have seen you, and now they glow red.

You jump up and spot the button on the control board marked DOORS. You reach for it but see SOL turn his blasters toward you, and you duck back behind the chair.

PFZAT! An energy explosion sounds in your ears. The wall beside you bursts into flames. The blast just missed you! Whew!

You look back and see that Gogol hangs from SOL's arm by his rubbery hands.

"You worthless gnat!" SOL flings Gogol away behind some crates and aims his blaster. "Now nothing can stop me—"

But you jump up, press the button, and dive behind a console before he can fire.

The doors to the Life Support Room slide open, and Chief Swift and his men storm the room, spraying it with energy beams. Several hit SOL's circuit board, melting it into a plastic blob. The robot stands motionless.

When the smoke clears, Swift sees you and Gogol looking at SOL's frozen form.

"Wh-where did you two come from?" he stammers, surprised.

You point to the air duct and smile. "We just dropped in."

THE END

"I'm going back, Gogol!" you holler over your intercom. You fire your jetpack at full thrust.

"Right behind you!" Gogol shouts as he does the same.

POW! The two of you collide and send each other sprawling in opposite directions away from the star station. The space monster roars, and then SOL laughs viciously.

It's a long, long time before you find your way back to the star station.

THE END

"If something **is** wrong with that security robot," you think to yourself, "he could cause trouble on the star station."

"Commander Brant?" you call as he hurries down the hall. You tell him about the security robot's strange actions.

He looks thoughtful and murmurs, "With problems in the Computer Room, we don't need a security bot that doesn't work right."

He says to the four of you, "We'd better check this out. I'll tell the Computer Room manager that we'll be a few minutes." He speaks into his wrist radio for a moment. Then you follow him down the hall.

As you walk, you pass a door marked ROBOT TEST AREA. "Could the robot have gone in here?" you ask.

"Let's see," the commander says. He opens the door.

As you enter the test area, your mouth drops open. "If I didn't know we were still in a star station, I'd think we were on our home planet, Nedram," you say.

A pretend sun shines from a bright blue sky in an enormous room. Strange plants cover

rolling hills and valleys. Flowers as big as
trees grow here and there, and odd birds fly
among their petals.

"This is where we try out all our new
robots," Commander Brant explains. "It's a
combination of different alien environments
in one room. We try to match it with the
places where our robots might be sent."

Nanny Robot circles in delight. "I was
perfected in a place like this."

BZZZT! An odd noise disturbs the quiet.

From behind a big rock steps a little
green-skinned, bald-headed alien wearing a

glass bubble helmet. Close behind rolls the huge security robot you saw at the shuttle.

"Sniksil, what's going on?" Commander Brant calls to the alien.

"I'm trying to fix—"

But before the little fellow can finish, the robot stops, raises his arm, and aims it at a boulder. Orange beams come from his fingers, BZZZT! and blast the boulder apart.

"Stop it, SOL!" Sniksil shouts at the robot.

"SOL, here, is our SOLAR Robot" Brant explains. "He's our special security robot. Sniksil is his creator."

The robot fires a blast that splits a tree.

Brant frowns. "Maybe you should disconnect him for now, Sniksil."

SOL turns and fires a bolt at Nanny. She short-circuits in a burst of sparks. SOL turns this way and that, firing all the time. Like everyone else, you dive for cover.

"Sniksil!" Brant hollers. "Do something!"

You peek from behind a rock and see the little alien chase after the huge robot.

SOL suddenly spins, picks up Sniksil, and tosses him across the room. With a SPLASH! the green alien lands in a shallow pond. SOL heads for the door. But instead of opening it, he bursts through the wall beside it and disappears up the hallway.

Commander Brant chases after the robot, shouting orders into his wrist radio. Carell, Gogol, and Rama start to follow him.

If you want to follow them and try to capture SOL, turn to page 60.

But if you think you should check on Sniksil's condition first, turn to page 51.

"Rama!" you shout. "Head for the workshop!"

The two of you jump through the doorway into darkness. Rama's Yazirian eyes see more in the dim light than yours. She takes your hand and leads you around boxes and crates that you can feel but not see.

Rama stops. "I can't see any other door!"

"Come on. There's got to be another way out of here." You squint, trying to see.

"No!" Rama cries. "We're trapped!"

You look back at the door you came in and see the evil soldier standing guard.

THE END

"Rangers!" you call out as your friends head through the hole in the wall. Rama turns, but Gogol and Carell must not hear you, for they follow Commander Brant up the hallway.

"What's the matter, Chaylo?" Rama asks.

"We've got to check on Sniksil."

"You're right! I'd forgotten about him." Rama runs toward the pond with you.

"Are you all right, Sniksil?" you ask, reaching out a hand to the little alien.

"No, I'm not!" Sniksil grabs your hand, and you pull him to shore. He's dripping wet. "I built that fool robot!"

"Why did he run off?" you ask quietly.

Sniksil looks away. He mumbles, "I put a part of him in upside down."

You and Rama exchange glances.

"I didn't think it would make that **big** a difference," Sniksil continues.

He plops down next to a giant flower and begins to cry with a strange hiccupping sound. The tears fog up his glass helmet.

You sit down next to him, not knowing what to say. Suddenly, he stops crying when he sees Perky on your wrist.

"Can I see that?" he asks, pointing to your Personal Radio Computer Kit.

"Sure," you say, unstrapping Perky.

Sniksil examines Perky, flips it over, and opens the back panel. The tiny circuit board glistens in the artificial sunlight.

"I've got an idea," he says as he takes a tool kit from his pocket. You start to worry when he sticks a tiny screwdriver into Perky's insides.

With a spark, Perky lets off a shrill whistle. You and Rama cover your ears as Sniksil grins triumphantly.

"Don't wreck it!" you shout.

The shrill noise from Perky gets louder until it sounds as if it's going to explode.

You grab Perky from Sniksil's hands. The whistle stops as suddenly as it began.

"Wait," Sniksil pleads. "I can use it to bring SOL back. Please trust me."

If you don't trust Sniksil with Perky, then keep it and turn to page 54.

If you do trust Sniksil, then give Perky back to him. Turn to page 56.

"Sniksil, Perky was a gift from my uncle," you tell the little alien. "My parents told me to take care of it. I'd rather keep it for now."

THUL-DOOOOM!

Through the hole in the wall, SOL rolls back into the Robot Test Area.

"Who was making that terrible screech?" he booms. His eye sensors glow red.

Spotting Perky in your hands, he snaps, "You're the one!" With a burst of speed, he moves toward you. You start to run away.

"Look out!" Rama cries, but too late.

The huge robot lifts you from the ground and drops you on top of a giant flower.

"That should keep you from bothering me!" he hisses. Then he rolls back out the hole.

Fear turns to anger as you scramble down the flower stem. "Let's go after him, Rama!" you cry.

The two of you leave Sniksil and race out of the test area. Soon you've caught up with Commander Brant, Carell, and Gogol.

Please turn to page 60.

You hand Perky to the alien.

"I'll be careful," Sniksil promises.

"Here we go again," shouts Rama as the whistle sounds from your wrist computer.

Just when you think your eardrums will pop, the wall bursts apart, and in rolls SOL.

Shaking, Sniksil lets go of the button on Perky, and the whistle stops.

"Very clever," SOL's voice booms. "You knew I couldn't keep away from that noise!"

"I-I designed you," Sniksil stutters, "and I'm going to stop you!"

"And how," SOL mocks, "are you going to do that?" He grabs hold of a tree, pulls it up

by its roots, and tosses it across the room.

"B-by disconnecting you," Sniksil's little voice cracks.

SOL laughs and then snarls, "Just try it!"

Though terrified, Sniksil takes a step toward SOL, but he stumbles over a plant root and falls. Perky flies out of his hand and lands at your feet. You grab it, and the noise starts again.

"AARRGGHHH!" SOL snarls. "Stop that!"

You turn up the volume, and SOL starts to roll toward you and Rama. You back up SMACK! into the stem of a giant flower.

"Let's get out of here!" cries Rama, and

she quickly scrambles up the flower stem.

"Now I've got you," SOL roars at you. He takes aim with his blasters.

Suddenly, Rama drops from her hiding place on the flower top onto SOL's head. She covers his eye sensors with her hands.

"I can't see!" SOL angrily reaches for Rama, but she dodges his mechanical hands.

Keeping the shrill sound going, you see Sniksil rise and sneak up to SOL's control panel. Bracing himself, he pulls at SOL's circuit box. But before he can break it completely free, SOL's upper body twists and knocks the little alien to the ground.

You dash over to take Sniksil's place. Ducking under SOL's swinging arms, you pull with all your might, and POP! the little circuit box comes loose in your hands.

SOL goes still as a statue.

"We did it!" Rama hoots from SOL's shoulders. "We stopped the SOLAR Robot!"

"For a Star Ranger, it's all in a day's work," you say proudly.

THE END

The rubble from bashed-in walls litters the hallway and makes it tough for you to follow Commander Brant.

Rama lets out a long whistle. "That SOLAR Robot sure does make a mess."

"How can one robot do this much damage?" Gogol asks in amazement.

"Easily," says Carell. "He was supposed to be the best security robot ever."

"So we gave him the best weapons we could make," Brant adds gloomily.

"Can we help in some way, sir?" you offer.

Brant smiles. "Thanks, Chaylo, but—"

A shriek comes from a nearby laboratory,

and the roar of energy blasts echoes down the corridor. You duck automatically.

"Now what?" Brant says, sighing. "That can't be SOL. He must be two or three levels away from here by now."

You all rush to the laboratory door and peek inside. You can't believe your eyes, for standing next to a computer terminal is a nine-foot-tall robot soldier!

The soldier turns toward the door. An energy bolt blasts at you and just misses.

You all duck back into the hall. Brant grabs a portable intercom with a video screen.

"Chief Swift! What's going on?" Brant

demands. "We've got a robot soldier here shooting at us. You're the chief security officer. Can you tell me where he came from?"

You can see the face on the screen frown. "I don't know, sir. They're all over the SOLAR Star Station. I'm sending out as many guards as I can to stop them."

"Let me know if you need any more help," Brant says. He switches off the intercom.

You know the Star Rangers should do something to help. But what? And where?

You could all help Chief Swift at the Life Support Room. Or you could split up to cover more territory. Gogol and Carell could stay with the commander, while you and Rama go back to the Robot Test Area and ask Sniksil for his help.

You decide to go to the Life Support Room. Turn to page 18.

You and Rama return to the test area, find Sniksil, and go with him to the Robot Workshop. Turn to page 64.

"Where did the soldiers come from?" you ask Sniksil. "We've seen them everywhere."

Sniksil bustles around his cluttered workshop. "I think they're SOL's."

"How can they belong to SOL?" you ask.

"Here, let me show you," Sniksil says. "I found this robot with her circuits burned out."

"Hey!" you cry, pointing at the bot. "That's Nanny Navigator Robot! She belongs to us!"

"Really?" says Sniksil as he fiddles with some of Nanny's switches. "Now she's good as new—better, after I fixed a few things."

He reaches inside Nanny's control panel and suddenly, an evil soldier appears before you!

"Look out, Chaylo!" Rama shouts.

"Oh, he can't hurt anyone," says Sniksil.

He puts his hand in front of one of Nanny's light sensors, and the soldier disappears. "It's a hologram."

"A hologram!" you say, snapping your fingers. "Just like the slimy creature we saw at the exhibit when we first arrived."

Rama frowns. "But what about the energy blasts those evil soldiers fired?" she asks.

"There are two light sensors set in the wall or computer terminal," Sniksil explains, "one to project the soldier image and the other to fire the blasts."

"Can we find SOL through the soldier holograms?" you ask.

"There are too many light sensors in this station," says Sniksil. He sighs.

As you look Nanny over, a thought comes to you. "Nanny can!" you say excitedly.

You open Nanny's control panel and punch in her tracking program. Her lights flash on, and she rolls to the door.

"Nanny's tracking function should lead us right to SOL," you explain. "After all, she is a **navigator** robot!"

"Come along!" says Nanny's crisp voice.

You all scurry after her down the hallway until a small figure appears ahead of you.

"Who's that?" Sniksil whispers.

You peer at the shape and see someone with brown hair and wearing pajamas.

"That's me!" you cry. Rama giggles.

You see that the picture is being projected from Nanny's light sensors.

Sniksil shrugs. "The picture must have been stored in your robot's memory."

Rama turns to you. "Maybe SOL's energy blasts messed up Nanny's tracking program. She could be leading us into a trap, Chaylo!"

"No!" cries Sniksil. "I fixed her."

If you still want to follow Nanny to SOL, turn to page 72.

If you'd rather turn back and find Commander Brant and the others, turn to page 68.

"I don't want to take any chances," you say. "Let's go back and look for Commander Brant. Maybe he's already found SOL."

"Suit yourself," says Sniksil. "I'm staying with Nanny Robot. Good luck."

You and Rama go back down the passage and follow it for a long time—too long. You're just about to suggest turning back, when you notice that Rama is floating a few inches off the ground. Then you realize that your feet no longer touch the floor!

As you begin to tumble head over heels, you see a sign that reads:

CAUTION: GRAVITY–FREE ZONE!

"Now they tell us!" you moan.

Below the sign there is a door labeled ESCAPE POD. Rama's fingers grab a ledge on the wall opposite the door. She reaches out to you, but you're just out of her grasp.

Floating helplessly five feet above the floor in the center of the corridor, what will you do?

"Don't panic, Rama!" you shout. "Just push off the wall gently and knock me to the pod door." Turn to page 70.

"My gravity boots!" you yell. "I can use them to get us down." Turn to page 71.

"What can we do in the escape pod?" Rama asks as she spins in the air.

"Radio for help," you explain.

"All right," Rama says. "Here I come." She pushes herself off the wall toward you.

"I said **gently**!" You shout too late. Rama slams into you hard, and you both fly into the pod door. It opens, and you tumble through, banging into the control panel.

"Nice shot!" you say. "I told you—"

The door bangs shut, and the sign POD ACTIVATED starts flashing. Rocket thrusters shake the pod and blast you off into space.

By the time you return the pod to the star station, it's too late for you to help.

THE END

"Gravity boots?" says Rama. "Why didn't you think of them before?"

"I was dizzy from spinning," you reply.

Bending over to reach your boots starts you somersaulting again. But you grab the dial on one boot and turn it down. Then you do the same with the other. In seconds, you're standing safely on the floor!

"Much better," you say, sighing.

"Hey! What about me?" Rama calls.

You reach up, grab her hand, and pull her along the hallway. Gradually, the gravity returns to normal, and Rama's feet touch ground again. You adjust your boots.

Without further delay, the two of you race back to Sniksil and Nanny Robot.

Trusting Nanny, you follow her quickly to a section of the SOLAR Star Station that is marked OFF LIMITS! Soon you enter a giant room labeled POWER ROOM. It's lined with generators and huge circuit panels.

As you stare, you hear a great rumbling. Out from behind a solar generator rolls SOL!

The yellow metal of his body glows as bright as a sun. His eye sensors burn red, and tiny sparks of blue light flash back and forth across his mouth speaker.

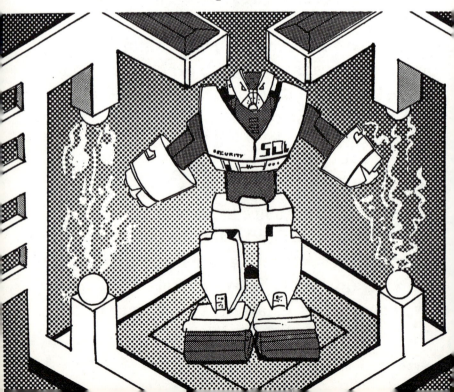

"Ah!" booms SOL. "So you came to witness my great energy surge. You weaklings! Soon I will be linked with the star station's solar generator, and then I, the SOLAR Robot, will have all the power!" His shrill laughter makes you shiver.

The robot turns and pulls cables from his own control box. Then he begins to wire himself directly to the solar panel collectors.

"What can we do?" whispers Rama.

You look at Nanny Robot and get an idea. "We'll frighten him," you say.

"That big robot? You're crazy!" Rama whispers. But Sniksil nods in understanding.

You keep an eye on SOL as Sniksil fusses with some buttons on Nanny Robot.

"We'll project the hologram of me that Nanny sent out before in the hallway. Only this picture will be huge!" you explain.

Suddenly, a thin beam of light shoots out from Nanny, and an enormous Chaylo stands in the center of the Power Room!

Rama gasps. Even **you** are startled by the giant image of yourself!

Hearing Rama, SOL turns toward you, sees

the huge hologram, and rolls back in horror.

While Sniksil keeps increasing the size of your image, you and Rama crawl around the right side of the hologram toward SOL. The robot's so frightened by the big Chaylo that he doesn't notice you.

As you creep behind SOL, your hand touches something cold and hard on the floor. It's a long, thick metal rod. You look up at the robot and notice that he keeps backing away from the hologram.

"Help me with an idea," you whisper to Rama. She nods.

Taking a deep breath, you each pick up one end of the rod. Then you kneel and hold it just behind SOL's big metal legs.

Again the huge robot rolls back. CLUNK! He hits the metal rod. The jolt nearly knocks you from your knees.

SOL tilts back, forward, to one side, and then lands CRASH! on his back. All the cables are ripped from his control panel. Sparks fly, and then SOL goes dark.

"Hooray!" you and Rama shout.

Sniksil jumps up and down with glee. "We

did it! We stopped SOL!" he cries. "Now I've
made up for my mistake!"

"What mistake?" you ask the alien.

Sniksil looks sheepish. "When I was
making SOL, I put a part in upside down."

You look at Rama, and you both laugh.

"Well, Sniksil," you say, "maybe now you'll
get a chance to make SOL something less
dangerous than a security robot. Maybe he
could be a gardener in the alien environment
of the Robot Test Area!"

THE END

FANTASY FOREST™ Books

ιs your dragon dragging?

Do you both need to go on an adventure?

Why not PICK A PATH TO ADVENTURE™
with these FANTASY FOREST™ Books?

- #1 THE RING, THE SWORD, AND THE UNICORN
- #2 RUINS OF RANGAR
- #3 SHADOWCASTLE
- #4 KEEP OF THE ANCIENT KING
- #5 DUNGEON OF DARKNESS
- #6 STAR RANGERS AND THE SPY
- #7 CASTLE IN THE CLOUDS
- #8 STAR RANGERS MEET THE SOLAR ROBOT

From the producers of the DUNGEONS & DRAGONS® Game

ENDLESS QUEST® Books
From the producers of the
DUNGEONS & DRAGONS® Game

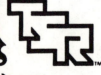

For a free catalog, write
TSR, Inc.
P.O. Box 756, Dept. EQB
Lake Geneva, WI 53147